MY SUPER COOL FRIENDS

MIS AMIGOS SUPER FABULOSOS

Illustration by Luciano Martinez • Illustrado por Luciano Martinez

Lectura Books
Los Angeles
www.LecturaBooks.com

I have the coolest friends at school.

En mi escuela tengo los amigos
más fabulosos.

Sofia is **round** like the moon.

Sofia es **redonda** como la luna.

Richard is **square** like a building block.

Richard es **cuadrado** como un bloque de construcción.

Mara is **tall** and **skinny** like a willow tree.

Mara es **alta** y **flaca** como
un arból sauce.

Matt is **small** like his Chihuahua.

Matt es **pequeño** como su chihuaua.

Ana is sometimes **angry** like a lion.

Ana a veces está **enojada** como un león.

Maddie is **sweet** like flowers.

Maddie es **dulce** como las flores.

Nelly has **curly** hair.
Nelly tiene el pelo **enrulado**.

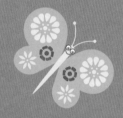

James has **straight** hair.
James tiene pelo **lacio**.

Isabella is **quiet** like a mouse.

Isabella es **tranquila** como un ratón.

Mario is **loud** like a drum.

Mario es **ruidoso** como un tambor.

Betty is **hot** like the sun.

Betty es **caliente** como el sol.

Jonathan is **cold** like a popsicle.

Jonathan es **frío** como un helado.

And then there's me, at school, with all my **super cool friends**!

Y luego estoy yo, en la escuela, ¡con todos mis **amigos super fabulosos**!

Publisher's Cataloging-In-Publication Data
(Prepared by The Donohue Group, Inc.)

Names: Martinez, Luciano, 1974- illustrator. | Lectura Books PreK Team.
Title: My super cool friends = Mis amigos super fabulosos / [Lectura Books PreK Team] ; illustration by
    Luciano Martinez = [Lectura Books PreK Team] ; illustrado por Luciano Martinez.
Other Titles: Mis amigos super fabulosos
Description: Los Angeles : Lectura Books, [2016] | Bilingual. English and Spanish on opposing pages. |
    Summary: A story about friendships in school and what's so special about each friend.
Identifiers: ISBN 978-1-60448-012-2
Subjects: LCSH: Friendship–Juvenile fiction. | Bilingual books. | CYAC: Friendship–Fiction. | Spanish
    language materials–Bilingual.
Classification: LCC PZ7.1 .M97 2016 | DDC [E]–dc23

Lectura Books
1107 Fair Oaks Ave., Suite 225, South Pasadena, CA 91030
1.877.LECTURA • www.LecturaBooks.com

Printed in Malaysia • TWP • 2016